T0090753

Education and Other Lies

Mary Meillier

iUniverse, Inc.
New York Bloomington

Education and Other Lies

This is a work of fiction. All of the characters, names, incidents, organizations, and dialogue in this novel are either the products of the author's imagination or are used fictitiously.

iUniverse books may be ordered through booksellers or by contacting:

iUniverse
1663 Liberty Drive
Bloomington, IN 47403
www.iuniverse.com
1-800-Authors (1-800-288-4677)

ISBN: 978-1-4401-7291-5 (sc)
ISBN: 978-1-4401-7292-2 (ebk)

Printed in the United States of America

iUniverse rev. date: 11/23/2009

Prologue

"Ma, I'm going to be a middle school teacher," said I.

To which she replied, "You're killing me. What will people think? Twelve years of private school education. Four years of college. And for what? This?"

"Ma, it's education, not the army."

"So what's wrong with the army? It's not a bad idea. Good pay, leave, retirement. . ."

"Ma, people in the army carry guns. They KILL people, Ma. They GET killed!"

"Don't confuse the issue," she replied.

INTRODUCTION

And so with the blessings of my family, I went into teaching. And I say, "went into," because it has proven to be a true arena. But let me start from the beginning. I applied for my teaching certificate with the Department of Education in Tallahassee, Florida. Now I am certain they received my application along with the other 30,000 each year with about as much enthusiasm as the Poles received Hitler. Yet they did respond in a record two months. However, it seemed I lacked one essential credit, "Special Methods of Teaching Secondary School Social Studies." I was hired temporarily until I fulfilled this requirement and the state gave me a generous amount of time to do this----forever.

My position was new, that of teaching Social Studies using computers. Barry University offered a course, "Special Methods of Teaching

Secondary School Social Studies Using the Computer." Wow, I must be living right! I called Tallahassee and asked if they would accept this course as my requirement. To this they replied, "Sorry, it's unacceptable." And all this without even a supervisor's help. This falls under the "I should have known then" department. An old song said, "It's a Barnum and Bailey world." I think it's an Allen Funt world. The only thing missing is the camera.

Yet I felt grateful. After all, I was hired to teach history and, in fact, I had only taken two courses during my entire four years of college. But who was I to argue with bureaucracy? In short, I took the gift and ran. As a student of mine told me one year, "Teachers are stupid. They just have the Teacher's Edition." Well, I did have the Teacher's Edition. So now I qualified to be stupid.

I started my first job as a sixth grade World Culture teacher during the middle of the year. Was I ever eager. Young minds to mold. Young futures to shape. Kind of just makes you break out into goose bumps. Yeah, this was for me! Making the world safe for democracy. My classes awaited. Never once did I wonder why

I was their third teacher since August. Never once did I question why I, a first year with no experience teacher, was being hired so quickly upon entering the field. But as quickly as the sun slips over the horizon I was to learn.

Remember Kotter and his SweatHogs? No contest. My students were pro's. The first week I was there six of my students had court dates. I thought their fathers were attorneys. Most students were shaving, boys AND girls. Not to worry. I was there. I would make the change in their miserable little lives.

Super teacher springs into action! My first assignment was an art project. Most listened very nicely. Then we divided the crayons and (Oh, God, let me forget) the scissors. This was a "shut up, no you shut up" society. Apparently they didn't learn everything they needed to know in kindergarten. Yet I did manage to force a workable system. Interestingly enough the students had rather unique ideas. Some wore their crayons. Others stuffed them in their ears. But, ah, the scissors. That was the moment. One student said, "Gee, this is the first time anyone ever let us have scissors." I started to stiffen. (Somehow "oops" didn't seem like quite enough.) Scissors took on a whole new meaning for me. They cut paper. They cut crayons. They cut clothes. They cut textbooks. They cut with a vengeance not seen since "Revenge of the Mole People." Grateful that anatomy had been spared, I retired the scissors as the students (and I use the term in its broadest concept) cried, "Aw, what'd ya go and do that for? We wuz just learnin' sumpin'."

Yet let me not have you think that students are the only characters out there. There is, of course, the ADMINISTRATION. Most administrators are basically teachers who escaped. Most of their time is spent trying to assure us that "they know where we're coming from." All the others in these offices are people who had the sense never to be a teacher in the first place. And never is there a day without festivity in these offices. Students bleeding, parents screaming, computers clicking and food abounding. Never have I visited this building that I am not reminded of the Piccadilly Cafeteria. Always there is the sweet aroma of freshly baked Danish, mouth-watering pizza, sizzling fajitas, or the like. We may not beat the Asians in Math, but we sure outsmell them. We often can't locate a student, be we can quote the entire Lo Chin menu by heart. We often can't get a student's home number, but we have Hungry Howie's on speed dial. I love priorities. I knew I was going to fit in well here.

Anyone who has raised a child, seen a child being raised, or has been a child should be able to understand that there is no book that can prepare you for everything. Teachers are called "professionals." We don't say a professional doctor, or a professional lawyer. We do, however, say professional wrestlers, professional linemen, etc. Since I consider education a contact sport, I guess we are professional teachers. This book is meant to poke fun at all of us. If you find yourself among these pages, you're in good company. We're all here somewhere.

Faculty Meetings

Now this is education at its finest. The moment when 150 great minds come together to solve the problems of education. Right! We begin with the time. Most of the staff has yet to figure out when the 8:00 meeting is. So . . . we wait for them. This usually takes about ten minutes. Okay with me. I'm a social animal. Standard excuse: I didn't know where the meeting was. (The faculty meeting has been in the band room since 1955.) Then another few minutes to get everyone to quiet down. (The excitement of meeting adults is just too much.) Now we have approximately seventeen minutes remaining for 150 people to discuss approximately thirty-two agenda topics. Ah, the "Agenda."

Let's move on the "Agenda." Never since Bounty, the-Quicker-Picker-Upper has paper been used so wisely. Not just 150 sheets of paper, but 300 (notice how quickly I did that) sheets of paper. Why? Because someone (who shall for now remain nameless, but hints will be given) hasn't figured out that one line doesn't have to be continued on a second sheet. Someone doesn't speak "font." So we sit in the band room, in chairs meant for munchkins, juggling purses, coffee cups, briefcases, student folders, and the "Agenda." A true work of art the "Agenda." It consists of approximately thirty-topics as I mentioned, most of which are held over from last week's meeting. And there are standard topics on the "Agenda" each meeting. My favorite is "STANDING AT YOUR DOOR." Teachers are to stand at their doors during the exchange of classes to ensure a calm transition. (So nobody piano-wires somebody.) Now this sometimes comes under the heading "Liability." Sometimes it's cleverly disguised as "responsibilities, teacher." Sometimes, under duress, it screams "**LOCK OUTS**!" I'm a little partial to that one. It must be the Bugsy Moran side of me. There's a story here somewhere. But I digress. I like to guess **where** "standing at your door" is going to be on the "Agenda." Once I guessed "8." It was "16." My friend Sharon said I was half right. And she isn't even "Math." (Teachers are referred to by their subject area – Oh yes, you're "Math!" No problem, I rather like anonymity myself.) I say let's just find the people NOT standing at their doors and hang them. This would effectively remove one item from our "Agenda." I get my efficiency from my mother the drill sergeant. My mother was the epitome of efficiency. Mealtime was her forte. We were a family of eight. One of my sister's friends once said, "The Russians could be marching down Eugene Street and Mrs. Manley would have dinner on the table at 5:30." And no matter what you did, it could be improved upon. Sitting? Standing? My mother would say, "Never stand when you can sit. Never sit when you can lie."

After about 700, "Ok, teachers, let's get quiet," we are now ready to move on to item 7 of the "Agenda." Oops, too late, the bell rings. Ah but is it really too late? "Let's just hurry and finish, teachers." What? Hurry and finish twenty-six items. You don't have to be "Math" to figure out we took seventeen minutes to complete six items. This is what I like to call the "Abbott and Costello" mathematical approach to time management.

An interesting aside to this mania is that all the students are now assembled at their respective "doors" for admission to class, another opportunity to awaken their minds and hearts. Bear in mind that we have students who check the teacher absentee board in the front office to see who's not coming today. Our gifted darlings have also cleverly figured out that Tuesday is "FACULTY MEETING DAY." Nothing gets by them. When the bell rings and no teacher is around for miles, guess what? "FREE DAY!" And now the fun really begins. Sixth graders are usually the victims. Jut ripe for a quick hit and run. These little latent felons have by mid-term figured out that Tuesday is a day to be reckoned with, but they're not quite sure how. Not to worry. The seventh and eighth graders are there. Things start to disappear: booksacks, lunches, money, sometimes even a student or two. However, bathrooms are the biggest targets. I read once where prison inmates write petitions to the court and sue for compensation (all free of course) for lots of sound reasons. Reasons such as: their ice cream melts, sandwiches are soggy, TV reception is poor, etc. I'm in the process of writing a grant to determine the relationship between bathroom graffiti and faculty meetings.

Seems nobody else has figured out when this happens or why. I bet the government would fund it, too.

Teachers, be at your doors promptly. . .

MORNING ANNOUNCEMENTS

Morning announcements are truly necessary. You need to know any important events happening on campus that day. Announcements will start promptly at 8:30, during homeroom. I have now learned to translate "officese."

WHAT THEY SAY
WHAT THEY MEAN

1. "Promptly at 8:30."
Whenever they're ready.

2. "Teachers, listen up, this important."
Nobody listened yesterday.

3. "Good morning, students and teachers."
Shut up and listen.

4. "It's a beautiful day here in South

Florida."
What the hell am I doing here?

5. "Students, we want you to be your best."
They've vandalized the bathrooms again.

6. "We're family here at our school."
Stop beating up the sixth graders.

7. "Students, we're proud of you."
Our jobs depend on your FCAT scores.
Please don't Christmas tree your answers.

8. "We've got a fine basketball team."
We lost.

9. "Boys (or girls), you did our school
proud."
We lost. Again

10. "I want to make this perfectly clear."
Does anybody out there speak English?

11. "We're repeating
yesterday's announcement."
And we're going to repeat it until somebody
listens.

12. “Today’s announcements will be brief.”
Principal’s out.

13. “We have a lot of important
announcements today.”
Principal’s in.

14. “We like to thank those teachers who
Walk their students to lunch.”
Those teachers not walking their students to
lunch will be fired – or worse – put out in
the portables.

15. “We’re having a problem on campus.”
Graffiti, vandalism, grand larceny . . .

16. “Students, we have a dress code here.”
You are not to come to school dressed for a
felony.

17. “There will be no hats on campus.”
Hat thief ring on campus.

18. “Teachers, when students leave the
room they must be accompanied.”
The military call this walking “point.”

19. “We have some of the finest

students here."
Nobody was arrested last week.

20. "We're very proud of the dedication of our teachers."
No subs.

21. "Don't forget."
You already did.

22. "Teachers, please check your mailboxes."
300 lbs of unread mail weighing the portable down.

23. "Students, enjoy your holiday."
Get lost.

24. "We welcome all parents to our PTA meeting."
We'd welcome ANY parent.

25. "There was a fine turnout for our PTA Meeting."
Someone showed.

26. "Please be prompt for the 8:00 meeting."

Faculty meeting at 8:15.

27. "Welcome back from spring break."
School's over.

28. "Teachers, Friday is not movie day."
Friday is movie day.

29. "Students are not to bring inappropriate equipment to school."
No guns or mace.

30. "One of our faculty will be out for an undetermined period of time. We wish her a speedy recovery."
"The Home" called.

31. "The emergency faculty meeting for tomorrow has been cancelled."
Gag order.

32. "Teachers, be sure you have contacted parents before failing a student."
Grade change forms in office.

33. "Boys must dress appropriately."
Holes in underwear are unacceptable.

"Girls must dress appropriately."
No hats, no navels, no thighs, no tight anything, no short anything, no sandals, no backless shoes, no colored hair, no excessive jewelry, no tanks, no tees . . .

34. "There is no prejudice at this school."
We hate everybody.

35. "There is a paper shortage."
Only the first 3,000 administrative memos will be copied and distributed to the immediate world.

36. "Teachers, challenge your students."
Paper shortage.

37. "We have applied for a grant."
Guinea pigs!

38. "We have been granted the grant."
Granted! Teachers to be taken for granted.

39. "We must do what's best for the students."
No raise.

40. “We are fortunate to have a resource officer on campus.”
There’s a man carrying a gun out there.

41.“We’d like to thank the teachers for the wonderful turnout at last night’s open house.”
Now aren’t you glad we made it mandatory?

42. “There will be no activity buses leaving at 5:30 today.”
Go home!

43. “Teachers, we must continue to do what’s in the best interest of the children.”
No raise again.

44. “Teachers, please disregard bells and hold your students in class.”
Lockdown!

45. “Students, have a wonderful summer.”
And we’ll be in Tahiti when your report cards arrive!

Fly me to the moon . . .

46. “Students, welcome back.”
Oh, God.

47. "Teachers, welcome back."
Check your emails, pick up your mail from mailboxes, get your rooms ready, pick up your supplies, pick up your keys, drop off your supply orders, submit your work orders, check out your laptops, sign in to the grade system, pick up your class rosters, sign up for your weekly workshops, submit your TDAs, turn in your updated profile, and don't forget the faculty meetings at 8:00 am and 3:00 pm. Have a nice day. (Anybody thinking of leaving early?)

STUPID QUESTIONS AND/OR STUPID ANSWERS

There are those who say that there are no stupid questions and no stupid answers. You be the judge.

1. Teacher: "Okay, students, the directions have been given. Are there any questions?"

Student: "Can you start over? I wasn't listening."

Suggested Teacher Response: "As soon as the others begin, come to my desk for more directed instruction."

What You Want To Say: "Why did you come today, for lunch?"

A prize will be awarded for the person who can correctly determine who had the "stupidest" question.

2. Teacher: "Now, please remember to put your complete name at the top of the page."

Student: "Do you want our last name, too?"

Suggested Teacher Response: "Yes, first and last names."

What You Want To Say: "No, I want to guess which "John" you are!"

Some people spend hours doing puzzles, others like to guess last names.

3. Student: "I was absent yesterday. Did you do anything?"

Suggested Teacher Response: "You may copy yesterday's assignment from the board."

What You Want To Say: "No."

I wonder if doing your nails counts?

4. Teacher: "Now, students, you have heard the complete story of the brave and short life of Anne Frank. Any questions?"

Student: "Can I go to the bathroom?"

Suggested Teacher Response: "Class will be over in five minutes. Can you please wait?"

What You Want To Say: "AFTER ONE OF THE MOST HEART-WRENCHING STORIES OF OUR DAY, YOU WANT TO GO TO THE BATHROOM? You want to know where you can go?"

If Hitler can't get your attention . . .

5. Teacher: "We have been discussing Egypt for two weeks. Now what continent are we on?"

Student: "North America."

Suggested Teacher Response: "True. Perhaps I didn't'word that correctly. On which continent does Egypt lie?"

What You Want To Say: "Egypt's continent, numbskull."

Well, I did say "we."

6. Teacher: "In honor of Valentine's Day, I have personally baked heart-shaped sugar cookies for you."

Student: "Aw, no chocolate?"

Suggested Teacher Response: "No, but I'm sure you will enjoy these."

What You Want To Say: "YOU are the reason people carry guns."

Anybody remember when "homemade" meant better than bought and "free" meant better than nothing?

7. Teacher: "Please take out your homework."

Student: "We had homework?"

Suggested Teacher Response: "Yes, it was on the board as it is everyday."

What You Want To Say: "I wrote the assignment on the board. We did HALF of them in class and YOU want to know if we had homework? No, WE didn't have homework, son. YOU HAD HOMEWORK! And guess what? You STILL have homework! And tonight you'll have MORE homework! This is America, son. Land of the free. Home of the brave. And here you sit, knowing nothing and having little hope of ever knowing any more. GET A CLUE!"

At times like this I thank the English language for having more words than any other language.

8. Teacher: "Where's your homework?"

Student: "I forgot."

Suggested Teacher Response: "Without the drill provided by the homework, you will have a hard time understanding and building on today's lesson."

What You Want To Say: "Did you forget to eat? Did you forget to bathe? Did you forget to dress? How do you forget to do something you do EVERYDAY?"

I always thought the ability to forget was a gift.

9. Student: (Asked during third quarter of school) "What time does school start?"

Suggested Teacher Response: "8:30. Check your student schedule given to you at the beginning of the year."

What You Want To Say: "If you're going to ask a stupid question, at least ask what time school ENDS!"

This is the big hand; this is the little hand . .

10. Student: "Can I put my sunflower seeds in the recycle bin?"

Suggested Teacher Response: "No, read the bin. It says only white paper."

What You Want To Say: "If I were your mother, when I finished with you there wouldn't be enough left to recycle."

See Jane. See Jane recycle. See Jane disappear into the hole in the ozone.

11. Teacher: "Everyone take out your number 2 pencil we gave you this morning. You must use a number 2 pencil."

Student: "Do we have to?"

Suggested Teacher Response: "Yes, the test calls for a number 2 pencil and cannot be scored using any other instrument."

What You Want To Say: "NO, PRICK YOUR FINGER AND WRITE IN BLOOD."

Day one of testing . . . only three more to go.

12. Student: "Are we doing anything today?"

Suggested Teacher Response: "The week's assignment is on the board as it is every day. And we always start each day with a writing prompt."

What You Want To Say: (Once again) "No."

My mother was right. Why didn't I go into the Army?

13. Teacher: "Students, remember that tomorrow is your Chapter Test. Please be sure to study your vocabulary words."

Student: "Do we have to study all of them?"

Suggested Teacher Response: "The test will cover all of the material in the chapter. Without knowing all of the vocabulary words, you will have a hard time understanding all of the concepts."

What You Want To Say: "No, pick out the ones you like, as will I."

Is it June yet?

14. Student: "Why'd I get an "F?"

Teacher: "Please take out your rubric. I listed all the items that needed to be covered. You can use this to "recheck" your paper."

What You Want To Say: "Why not?"

Maybe it's me!

15. Student: "When is this class over?"

Teacher: "Please check your school schedule for times." **OR** " Class will be over shortly." **Or** "Please continue working until I say "time's up."

What You Want To Say: "For you? When it started!"

Plop, plop, fizz, fizz . . .

16. Student: "Can we have a free day today?"

Teacher: "There are no 'free' days. We have a set syllabus and we must take advantage of all our time so we can be fully prepared for the upcoming tests and to ensure that you are fully prepared for the next grade."

What You Want To Say: "Sure." **Or** "Why not? The best things in life are free!" **Or** "Free! Free! Nothing's free, my friend." **Or** my favorite stand-by: "No."

SPECIAL ANNOUNCEMENTS

Things happen during the day that are without a doubt beyond our control and so it is often necessary to make special announcements. However, by the time afternoon arrives there is very little subtlety left --- in anybody. Some messages are known as "all-calls." A very endearing term that means, "we don't know where anybody is." This method allows the front office access to every classroom simultaneously. This is, of course, used for emergencies only. One day we had forty emergency all-calls and each one was preceded by "teachers, please excuse this interruption." If you consider there are five class periods, each forty-eight minutes long, that's one all-call every six minutes. I've known people with permanent tics who had more peace. A few classics, if you please.

1. "Mr. Comiskey, please buzz the front office with the location of your class."

He's been in room 24 for EIGHT years. If he's not there, chances are he's dead or ignoring them, or both.

2. "Teachers, please send the following students to (insert guidance, front office, student affairs, or assistant principal's office) at this time: Shanequa Williams, Shameka Smith, Mohammad Jerusalem, uh, uh, Erythromycin Jones, Shakima Louie, Yolanda Markham, Christopher Hullabaloo?, Hallaluia uh Johnson, Kareem Abdul Harris, Tommie Harris, Tammie Harris?, whoever, Ricardo Johanssen uh.. uh.. Ayokelne Olowyearen, uh, uh, Ramsumid Popka, Jesus Jacobs, Ariza Ariza – teachers that could be a mistake, Leeilani Wilson, Moses McSweeny, Chin Chan, what?, Cheech Somebody, uh, uh, uh, Katrizinka Wrizkazani, Carlos Montoya Goldstein, uh, uh, uhhhhh, Mishall Abednigo, John Paul Jones Martini, George Washington Martini, Shamika Williams, Shakima Williams, Handsome George . . . ten

second pause . . . Leo Leoli ..Leali.. Leaeli...Leo L.,Marian or Martin Stpeu, Mary Lou uh, uh, Mary Lou, uh, uh. If you have a Mary Lou Yosomething send her too, Michael Michel? Michael or Michel Quyintanescu, Susan Lyn Anne Theresa Stanislas Manley-Rome . . . Teachers I think that's one student but if not send them all and finally, Mary, I mean Matt Nelson, Ulysses S. Green, Myra Dyra, Louis Lewis, Alphonse Algonquin . , . uhuhuhuh. . . Abraham Lincoln O'Shaunnasey,Dimitri uhuhuuh Dimitri uhuhuh – Okay. Let me repeat. Teachers please send. . ."

Oh, God, please let me die now.

3. "Mrs. Meillier, if you're still on campus, please buzz the front office.

Are there instructions if I'm not?

4. "Teachers,we have a bus change: students who ride Bus 8679 will ride Bus 7968, and students who ride Bus 7968 will now ride with students from bus 8679. Let me repeat. Students . .

Isn't that clever? Students riding bus 7968 will ride bus 7968. Glad we cleared that up.

5. "Attention, students. All students MUST have a School Bus ID card to ride the bus home from school. If you don't have one, get on the bus anyway.

I MUST look up MUST in the dictionary.

6. "Teachers, the emergency faculty meeting has been cancelled. I repeat, the emergency faculty meeting has been cancelled. We will schedule another when we have time.

I don't know about you, but I always have time for an emergency.

7. "Please excuse the interruption. If you are driving a brown car, license plate 678XRG935, you have left your lights on."

This poor soul can't remember to turn her lights off. What makes anybody think she'll remember her license plate number?

8. "Mrs. Meillier?" they ask. "Yes," I reply. "Where are you?" they ask.

No I may be mistaken, but didn't THEY call ME? WHO am I, yes. Even WHY am I! But WHERE am I?

9. "Excuse the interruption, teachers." Nothing follows.

Nothing like a good interruption I always say.

10. "Teachers, I hate to bother you, but if you were scheduled for the assembly at 9:00, please disregard that memo. Please take your students to the 10:00 assembly. If you were scheduled for the 10:00 assembly please disregard that memo. Please take your students to the 9:00 assembly. If you were scheduled for the 11:00 assembly, please don't disregard that memo. Please take your students to the 11:00 assembly which has been moved to the gymnasium, except for those assemblies during lunch times which will be held in the gymnasium also, and except for those early assemblies

which will now be held tomorrow. Thank you."

No Problem.

11. "Mrs. Meillier, you have a phone call in the front office."

"See you, 32 students. I know you'll remain in your seats, doing what you're supposed to, hitting no one, stealing nothing, bothering not a single soul, just working quietly and intently on the most interesting of topics, "Cartograms Around the World."

12. "Attention, teachers. Tomorrow we will be having a surprise fire drill at 9:00am. Please tell your students."

Does the name "Gomer" come to mind?

13. "Mrs. Meillier, are you expecting a call?"

If I answer "No," does she hang up?

14. "Hello?" "Hello," I reply. "Hello," I reply again.

Hmm . . . maybe it's code. Maybe I shouldn't have been chasing that cockroach at yesterday's faculty meeting.

15. "Teachers, please excuse the interruption. We are testing the PA system. Please call the front office if you cannot hear this announcement."

Maybe if I turn up my Beltone I can hear it.

16. "Teachers, please disregard the bells. We are testing the fire drill bell. If there is a real fire, we will notify you by bell."

And that bell would sound like?

17. "Teachers, we hate to bother you again this afternoon. However, there will be no afternoon announcements today."

And what time is it now?

18. "Teachers, your grades were due at 9:00am. It is now 10:00am. Please try to have them in on time."

Hmm, see why the 8:00 faculty meeting starts at 8:15!

19. "Teachers and students, the following announcement is for you."

Really? I thought it might be for Congress.

20. "Teachers and students, please remember that tomorrow is a holiday."

No kidding! All of us had the holidays marked in August!

DIFFICULT STUDENTS

1. Students who don't do homework.

2. Students who don't remember to do homework.

3. Students who don't know there IS homework.

4. Students who don't "do" rules.

5. Students I like to refer to as the "BUT I JUST" students."

    a. Students sharpen pencils at the beginning of class and may not get up without permission. "But I just needed to sharpen my pencil," says student with pencil point sharp enough to etch glass.

b. Students may not talk during testing. "But I just asked for a pencil," says student with straight "F's," a rap sheet longer than the Dead Sea scrolls AND clearly wouldn't ask for a pencil when he could just steal it.
c. Students may not engage in any physical contact with another student. "But I just touched her." The touch requires a 911 call and 17 stitches.

6. The "Don't Touch Me" students. I think to myself, do I have "Stupid" stamped on my forehead. Most sixth graders don't believe in bathing or toothbrushing on a regular basis. Don't flatter yourself, kid. Let Ma Bell reach out and touch you.

7. The "Do we have to, are we going to be graded" students. Always a pleasure to reach an eager mind. I think of Mark Twain: all you have to do is pay taxes and die. Which will it be, kid?

8. The "I'm going to tell my mother" students. Now I try to be gentle here. Listen, son, tell it to the judge!

9. Students who argue with directions. Why do we have to do it on the computer? Why does it have to be so long? Do I have to include pictures? What if it's not on time? I quote my philosophical mother, "Because I said so." Hey, it worked for me.

10. Students who come late. All good excuses – There was a riot on the bus and the driver threw us all off – Dad got out of prison last night and we all stayed out late celebrating – My aunt died (two months ago) – My brudda woke up late and drove me late (lives two blocks away) – I got lost on the way to class (been in school two quarters) – Teacher kept us after class so we could be late and you would punish us. Ah the joys of teaching ..

CONFERENCES

Periodically it is necessary to have conferences, sometimes with students about students, and sometimes with parents about students. These following stories are true, only the names have been changed to protect the not-so-innocent.

Scenario One:

Teacher: "I'm so glad you could come. We're having problems with Alphonse's aggressive behavior."

Parent: "So what – I've had nothing but problems since he's been born and his father's even worse."

And you aint' no American Beauty rose either, sister.

Scenario Two:

Parent: "My child says she was punished because she refused to clap at a performance."

Teacher: "Yes, we are trying to teach students appropriate etiquette, both in and out of the classroom."

Parent: "Well, my child doesn't have to clap. I don't clap if I don't want. And she doesn't have to either. That's her right as an American."

I guess I missed the "right to be a jackass" in the Bill of Rights.

Scenario Three:

Teacher: "Your child took a watch that belonged to a teacher."

Parent: " Did you see him take it?"

Teacher: "He was wearing it."

Parent: "Did you see him take it?"

Teacher: "No."

Parent: "How do you know he took it?"

Teacher: "Well, first he said he found it in the bathroom behind a toilet. Then later he said he found it in the classroom under a stool that, by the way, doesn't exist. And he has a history of stealing things."

Parent: "So you can't prove he took it."

She's right. Circumstantial evidence like this almost convicted O. J.

Scenario Four:

Teacher: "Your child has a difficult time focusing."

Parent: "Huh?"

Apple doesn't fall far . . .

Scenario Five:

Parent: "I'm so sorry I'm late. My husband forgot his briefcase. The traffic was horrible.

Then I forgot my notepad so I could write down everything we talk about this morning, so I had to go back to the car. So, now! What's the problem?"

Teacher: "Your child has difficulty getting to class on time and frequently forgets his supplies."

His excuses are lame too.

Scenario Six:

Teacher: "Jonathan is very demanding of my time. He demands I stop and listen to him no matter what else is happening. His language is quite abusive when I cannot accommodate his wishes immediately."

Parent: "Well, what do you want him to do – kiss your as--?"

I was thinking more like sitting down, but ...

Scenario Seven:

Teacher: "Harold refused to do homework. He says he can pass the test just fine without it."

Parent: “So?”

Good point!

Scenario Eight:

Teacher: “Eustis does not complete most of his class assignments and never turns in his homework.”

Parent: “My child is very bright. He is bored with school and homework. He needs to be challenged.”

Teacher: “ He is indeed bright. Perhaps we should test him for the gifted program.”

Nothing like advanced work to make a non–worker work. All “bright” children figure their parents out double quick.

Scenario Nine:

Teacher: “Fred has had numerous absences this marking period and hasn’t turned in several of his assignments.”

Parent: "My child is afraid of you."

Teacher: "Perhaps we should have Fred here so we can get to the root of the problem"

Good, fear will keep him alive.

Scenario Ten: (Phone call)

Teacher: "I just called to tell what a delight it is to have Norman in my class."

Parent: "Ok, who is this?"

Sometimes I wonder myself?

FCAT

For those of you who don't live in Florida, FCAT stands for Florida Comprehensive Assessment Test. It's code for let's see how we can get re-elected by creating such a complicated testing program that people have to re-elect us just so we can get them out of the mess. It is my firm opinion that anyone who professes he is doing what is in the best interest of the child, will lie about other things. Everything in education revolves around money and politics, or politics and money, whichever comes first.

Now FCAT testing is in March, just enough time to get everyone in high school who hasn't been able to read for fifteen or sixteen years, reading. Ah, the sweet smell of success. And just to make sure that everybody is relaxed and comfortable with the process, we begin a daily countdown. Only 180 days until FCAT . . . only179 days until FCAT. Be still my heart.

We also put up signs around the campus . . . "Beat the FCAT." "NO FEAR FCAT." "Just Do It." (I think we stole that one.) Now I have an FCAT question for you. If you have 16 banners around the campus, and each banner costs $150, and you have two corporate sponsors who split the costs, how much does each banner cost?

a. $2400?
b. More than they want to pay?
c. Who cares?
d. Some of the above?
e. All of the above?

My grandchild, who is in kindergarten, came home and announced that she had FCAT homework. I asked her what FCAT was. (It's just the devil in me.) She said, "I dunno know. They told us, but I dunno know. I never see a cat." Guess what, Kid? Neither does anybody else in education. My other grandchild who is in the third grade asked, "Is school over after FCAT?" No, honey, it's just beginning.

So now we educators are getting into the swing of things. Everybody is reading, comprehending, and passing. Ah, ha! A red light goes off in the heads of our politicians. "They're getting the hang of this FCAT. We won't be necessary. We better change the rules." And so the games begin again. "Parents, we must continue to challenge our students." This is more "code." The test doesn't change, just the scoring. I used to play games like that with my younger sister. "Uh, uh. That was the rule yesterday. The rules today are different. Oh, too bad. You lose." The truth is, I've been preparing for FCAT my whole life!

And just so you don't think we only care about kids being able to read and compute, they have added "Science" testing into the equation. And sometime soon they're going to add Social Studies. One day we may actually address the whole child.

CERTIFICATION

Now here's a part of the educational process that I truly love. It's called certification and, for those of us who are already certified (certifiable?) re-certification. There is an entire staff of hundreds of people who are here to help us. Everyone who wants to teach MUST be certified. Every five years teachers must re-certify in order to continue to teach in the system. Now, there are several things to consider when certifying. All of this is conveniently located on the Department of Education's web page:

No Child Left Behind: acronymly known as NCLB. Leave it to rich Republicans to decide that after 230 years, we should leave no child behind.

Statement of Eligibility (SOE): heaven forbid we didn't have an acronym

Alternative Certification; this is for people who had the foresight NOT to become a teacher.

State Temporary Certificate: for those of you who want the chance to run!

State Professional Certificate Renewal: I wonder if there is one for Non-Professionals? No matter, it still costs $56, and an additional $30 if you're late! We all understand "TARDY." And DON'T do it early. Otherwise, all forms will be returned – except for the money order.

Reappointment/Termination Prevention: if I have to tell you how NOT to get terminated, I don't want you.

FTCE Exams: Florida Teacher Certification Exams. You must take a subject area examination (SAE), a Professional Education (PED), and a General Knowledge Test (GKT). We're not going to let any university tell US that their tests are better than ours. Harvard, Yale – Hah! At least we're consistent. We don't trust anyone! (We also don't take the results of any other state's certification tests. So there.)

Duplicate Certificates: what? Your school doesn't have a copy machine?

Incentive Awards: Not that educating young minds isn't its own reward. However, we want to make sure that our teachers are happy. Basic incentive is for those who have 15 semester hours and/or 300 in-service points beyond the Bachelor or Master's degree. And for this you get $2000 per year, before taxes. Then we have Advanced Incentive that is for teachers who have 30 semester hours and/or 600 in-service points beyond the Master's degree, or 15 semester hours and/or 300 in-service points and the Basic Incentive beyond the Master's degree and 10 years Florida teaching experience. And for this you receive $2700 a year, before taxes, assuming you understand it. In-service points need to have been earned in Broward-County-School-Board-approved in-service programs. Points transferred from another county are NOT acceptable except for ESOL, Gifted and Clinical Educator. Ah, the efficiency of consistency!

ESOL: Florida teachers are required by a Consent Decree to participate in training when they have a limited English proficient (LEP) student assigned to their classes. (I don't know who consents. Nobody asked me.)

Degree Stipends: as with any profession, the more education, the more money. A Master's degree nets you $3650, before taxes. And a doctorate gets you $8000. I wonder if we could afford health care for everyone if we paid medical doctors the same way!

Out-of-Field: It's hard enough to teach in-field. Is there someone who wants to teach something he doesn't know?

Professional Preparation Coursework: MUST have education courses. How can you teach ANYthing without this? But, alas, we do have alternative preparations! Hmm. . . . here's that special definition of MUST again.

Broward Certification: if we don't trust Harvard . . .

Charter Schools: Your current school isn't up to standard, check into the newest flavor. Nothing like a new, untested school that doesn't have to subscribe to the rules like the rest of us.

Endorsements/Subject Additions: not worth figuring out which form to fill out. Just teach out-of-field. It's easier to teach something you DON'T know than to try and add something you DO know. I have ESOL, Gifted and Middle Grades endorsements. I also have middle grades certification, so I'm not sure why I need to be endorsed. But I do feel special.

Today I received "hot topics" in certification. Seems that now we are dividing up the broad area of "Social Sciences" into four distinct areas. Now if you have been certified in one of these areas already, you are considered "highly qualified." Teachers who do not have a specific Social Science 5-9, Social Science 6-12, or middle grades integrated curriculum 5-9, or a HOUSE plan for each of the separate Social Science subject areas taught for either History, Economics, Geography, and/or Political Science are not considered highly qualified and must undergo more training/testing/certification. This is all part of NCLB. We're not leaving any kids behind, but teachers are another story. Again, I thank the Republicans for making education so complicated that death looks easy! I wonder how many Congresspersons have taken tests for competency . . . hmmm . . . I might be onto something here.

I had a friend who was a Science teacher for several years. He had all the required credentials: 4 year degree, passed the New Education Support System, in short, fully certified. He quit one day to become a law enforcement officer. I saw him back on campus 7 months later in full uniform with a gun on his hip. You have to wonder about a system that requires 4 years plus to learn to educate someone, but only 7 months to kill him.

BASIC AND ADVANCED INCENTIVE

The County is very generous with taxpayer money. For those of us who have continued our education past the Bachelor's degree, we can get what is called Basic Incentive or Advanced Incentive. You get Basic Incentive for 300 in-service hours past your last degree. However, if you get your Master's degree after you earn Basic Incentive, then you lose the Master's degree pay and receive on the Basic Incentive pay. Now you have to "re-earn" your Basic Incentive. Another 300 hours of in-service. However if you have your Bachelor's and your Master's degrees, you can get your Basic Incentive without losing any pay at all. Ah, but it's not over yet. If you have your Bachelor's, your Master's, and your Basic Incentive, then you can earn (after another 300 hours) your Advanced Incentive. Are you still with me? If not, don't worry. I'm beginning to lose myself.

I was told that I was 60 points shy of my credits for Advanced Incentive. All year, I worked at getting enough in-service hours to qualify. I applied and was told the following (direct quote):

"When your in-service was 'ran' in August 2006, the dates that it was 'ran' was from 7/1/1996 - 9/1/2006. You 'have' 240 in-service points during that validity period toward Advanced Incentive. Now that you are applying for the 07/08 school year, the points from 1996 'drops' off. Your in-service then ran from 7/1/1997 – 9/1/2007. Your total in-service points during that period 'are' 561. I then subtract the 300 points you used in 2003 for Basic Incentive. This will leave you with a total of 261 in-service points toward Advanced Incentive."

To make a long story longer, I needed 40 hours last year, and this year, after earning 97 new in-service points, I now needed 39 additional hours to qualify. And I thought I didn't understand Math?

WORKSHOPS

The District, through Human Resource Development (HRD), instituted its breakthrough "One Voice" Plan. This was designed to help everyone be the best teacher possible. The plan was (I say was for a reason you will understand later) composed of the Seven Correlates of Effective Schools, the Eight Step Instructional Process, and the Nine High Yield Strategies. In short, 7+8+9=ONE. I was thinking of having a t-shirt created, but I still had 2 years before retirement and I didn't want to spend them in a portable with the Sweathogs.

The truth is there were several other programs "inside" the One Voice. There were eight in all: the "One Voice" Instruction, The Seven Correlates of Effective Schools, The Eight Step Instructional Process, The Nine High Yield

Strategies, A Framework for Understanding Poverty, Classroom Walk-Through, CHAMPS, and Action Research. When all teachers working in the district level offices (not in a school), returned to work in July, they were given the generous time of one month to complete all of these workshops. Realizing that the possibility of completing eight workshops that hadn't all been scheduled yet might be impossible, everyone was given until December to complete the training. Just so you get an accurate picture of how well planned we were, I shall attempt a brief explanation of each program.

"One Voice" Introduction: This was designed so that, well, so that we all speak with one voice.

Seven Correlates of Effective Schools: Successful schools have seven correlates that make them successful. This is what I like to call "wake up and smell the coffee."

Eight Step Instructional Process: There are eight steps to ensure student success. Just because you have earned a degree in education, been awarded a formal state certification, and completed the New Teacher Support System program, it certainly doesn't mean you know how to instruct. Twenty years in the system and NOW I learn to instruct.

Nine High Yield Strategies: There are nine strategies you need to use while instructing to make sure that the instructing is successful. I think this may be a correlate, but I'm not sure. Maslow, eat your heart out.

A Framework for Understanding Poverty: Now this is my favorite. If the seven correlates, eight steps, and nine high yields aren't enough to confuse you, we must throw in poverty to muck up the situation. I wonder if we have to be taught to understand the wealthy? I'd VOLUNTEER for this one! I've been understanding poverty for awhile.

Classroom Walk-Through: This program is designed to teach you what administrators are looking for when they walk into your classroom. This has seven parts: T1, T2, T3, T4, SL, SLE, and LE. And this has nothing to do with the "7, 8, or 9." I like to call this "nanny nanny boo boo, we got you."

CHAMPS: In case the "7, 8, and 9," plus Poverty and Walk-Through can't make a teacher out of you, well we have Classroom Management, cleverly disguised as "CHAMPS." In the old days, we used to call this crowd control.

Action Research: Now this is a year-long program. I'm not sure what you do here, nor what you learn here, but if I'm careful I'll be retired before I have to find out. At my age, my idea of action research is a good book and a chilled Chardonnay. (This is also my new idea of "getting lucky.")

Now remember when I said "One Voice WAS?" Well, we now have a new Superintendent and we are no longer using the "One Voice" Plan. Nope, nope, nope. Don't know if it wasn't successful, or if it was a whim. I'm not sure what tense we're using now either, but who cares. One voice, forked tongue? Two years and counting.

We're also no longer using the term Senior Management. No, sirree. Now they are now the Executive Leadership Team. I feel much more empowered already. I'd much rather be lead than managed, but since they still tell me where to go, what to do and how to do it, I wonder . . .

WORKSHOP ETIQUETTE

It is important to remember that the "One Voice" workshops were designed especially to make sure that teachers are successful. In short, they were mandatory. And all teachers must know "THE RULES."

1. Everyone will be on time, except the instructor.

2. Instructors may change in mid-stream and may adjust the course as they see fit. You will be expected to know this without warning.

3. Homework can be sent by email, but a hard copy is needed for follow-up. (At least my mother didn't have to sign it.) The county is going green, but it's light green!

4. If you cannot attend the workshop because you are teaching the workshop, then you must arrange to attend later.

5. All lessons will be tailored to suit your work location. If homework requires the presence of students, find a co-worker. (And do what? They never tell you.)

6. They let you out early so you don't have to wait in the line while parents pick up their children. (HRD is conveniently located at the back side of the school's parking lot and parent pick-up route.) I now know that "early" isn't part of "my voice" because after eight hours in a workshop, I don't consider fifteen minutes "early."

7. All workshops start with "housekeeping." This is where you learn the rules. Some clever trainers let US make the rules. They usually don't make this mistake a second time.

8. There will be small bowls of candy on the tables to make you feel at home. I would prefer a bottle, preferably wine, but nobody asked me.

9. Lunch is always extended past the usual hour, but there is never any place to go.

10. Watches are always synchronized. Teachers, the time is . . . (I set mine with the U.S. Naval Observatory.)

11. All teachers who are here because they signed up sit at the front tables. All those who WERE signed up sit at the back tables. Since most of these workshops are usually held in portables, we live in the hope that the sound of the AC will comfort us and drown out the goody-two-shoes at the front tables.

12. To make certain that everyone is comfortable, we have two temperature settings: freezing and hell!

13. Workshops always have an "ice breaker" to make sure that we all get to know

each other. We all look forward to this as much as dry heaves.

14. All workshops end with "feedback" or "appraisal." If we appraise while at the workshop, everyone was super. If we appraise online at a later time . . . well, suffice it to say, I love anonymity. I may speak with one voice, but it's loud!

15. If you do not want in-service points, you do not have to complete the follow-up. (You would take these workshops for fun?)

16. Sometimes if you are late, they make you sing something aloud to the class. Hmmm, who's being punished here?

17. There's always a pre-test and post-test. (They are exactly the same.) Wouldn't ANYbody do better after learning something they never knew before, particularly if he had seen the questions?

18. You always have two breaks, one in the morning and one in the afternoon. Believe me, I broke long before either.

19. Workshop presenters are always so pleasant and agreeable. Can you spell a-p-p-r-a-i-s-a-l?

SUPERINTENDENT'S SCHOOLS

Some of our schools have a special designation. These are the schools that have had the misfortune to be graded by the State as a "D" or "F" school based upon their students' FCAT results. As if this isn't enough humiliation, they are now labeled Superintendent's Schools. This is code for "HE'S WATCHING YOU!"

Special programs have been put in place, designed to help these low-performing students pass the FCAT. One of my favorites is the "Pull Out" Tutoring Program. Those of us who are no longer in the classroom (some for twenty years), but still work for the School Board, were chosen to tutor select students in these schools. I'm all for tutoring, but I question the wisdom in putting me, who has had no math course since 1965, in a classroom to tutor students in math. It doesn't take a math person to figure out that this doesn't "add up." A second concern is this. These students have had anywhere from six to twelve years in school, and now in only eight weeks, two hours per week, I am going to make a difference in their test scores. Believe me if I could do that, I would be in consulting, not to mention on the *Today Show*.

Please understand that during this tutoring phase, our district was in a "budget freeze." No one in the schools was allowed to spend any money for anything unless it was approved by one of the Area Offices, or the Superintendent himself, and it MUST (here's that word again) be an essential service. Now I don't know about you, but I thought all teaching expenses were essential. Who could know! (Thank the heavens we had the oversight to "over" order on toilet paper.) But I digress.

During this tutoring phase, we were all paid extra: our hourly rate plus planning time and mileage. And now these students will be monitored to see just how much they have improved in these two hours per week, for eight weeks. So these children had sixteen hours (assuming, of course, they came) extra. Wonder what I could learn in sixteen hours that I hadn't been able to learn in seven years! At any rate, I just earned approximately $1500. Let's hear it for budget freezes. As my Momma used to say, "It's just as good in my pocket as theirs."

BUDGET FREEZE

Sounds simple, huh? Frozen, no movement, suspended state. Let's talk seriously about this "budget freeze." As I said, this means that all monies are frozen, both at the district level and at the school level. If you want something you must write a letter to the Area Director, accompanying the requisition request, explaining how this is ESSENTIAL to the school/program. Perhaps we were buying those $2000 toilet seats like the Federal Government.

Now as I understand it, money is so tight that we who have been out of the classroom doing other jobs that were advertised and promoted by the School Board, will now be returned to the classroom for the next school year and subsequent years should we still be alive. This ought to save the District about $2M. Sounds like a plan. However, some of us were being paid by federal grants, so no money was coming out of the operating budget for our salaries. Hmmm . . . I know this is going to save money because that's the Master Plan . . . just can't figure out how! Maybe I should have taken more math.

Now I should be fair here. We really weren't "returned;" we were, as the Superintendent put it, "realigned." And we shouldn't be upset, as a member of the Executive Leadership Team so eloquently stated, "What is your problem? You still have a job." Can't argue with that.

I lost my job once when I was working as an Administrative Aide for the East Baton Rouge Parish District Attorney in Louisiana. A new DA was in and I was out. The just ousted DA, formerly one of the most powerful men in the State of Louisiana, actually called me personally to express his sorrow and vowed to help me get another job suited to my talents. Now that's class. By the way, the newly elected DA was ousted from office for malfeasance. What goes around . . .

Yet once again I have digressed. Let's continue with what I consider another classic. Seems that the District will not replace anyone who quits a position here at the District offices. Nope, we must do without. AND remember, we are sending all teachers on special assignment back into the classroom so we don't have to hire any NEW teachers at the school level. Yet, AHA! We are advertising for a New Deputy Superintendent and SEVERAL Area Directors. Let me give you a little brief history. Teachers on special assignment (TSAs) were originally hired because the State of Florida said that the County was too top heavy. So we got rid of lots of positions "at the top" and replaced them with TSAs. Does "Catch-22" ring a bell? I figure I'll apply for all of these new positions. Why not? I think I might just be a shoo-in! Truly one has to appreciate the beauty of the bureaucracy in bureaucracy.

CONCLUSION

I started this book several years ago. During that time, lots of changes occurred. When I started teaching there was no FCAT, no Superintendent's Schools, no Executive Leadership Team, no laptops or computers in the classroom, no Windows®, no email, no cell phones – had enough?

But what we did have was FUN. My students learned to work most available computer applications, including desktop publishing. They learned a little of the languages of every culture we studied. They integrated art and music into their projects. They created cultural cookbooks. They laughed with each other. They cooperated and collaborated with each other. They learned to research and to validate their research. And every project culminated with a celebration of learning: a 40's "name that tune" program, a 50's sock hop and costume contest, a 60's t-shirt tie dye, a 70's sit-in, a Japanese rice-eating contest with chopsticks, a Chinese kite creating and flying contest, a family history tile that was secured to the outside hallways, and oh so many more. We wrote grants to cover the costs so everyone could participate without question.

What FCAT did was take the fun out of education. There were too many "eight" of this, "seven" of that, "nine" of the other. By the time you figured out HOW to teach, you weren't sure WHAT to teach. Not that the "eight, seven and nine" philosophies weren't sound. They were just too much, too quick, and certainly too late for most of us.

Yes, I have made fun of teachers, administrators, students, parents, just about everybody with whom I came into contact. And this is good. First is just feels plain good. Second, we need to take a look at ourselves as others see us. We need to lighten up. We need to freshen up. We need to remember what school is not about. It's not about politicians. It's not about money. It is about learning, and living, and experiencing. Politics should not drive our school system policies and practices. If everyone REALLY did what's in the best interest of the children, schools would not be holding fundraisers and dinners to support the curriculum. Teachers wouldn't have to write grants that require enough data to complete another degree. Schools wouldn't need someone just to look for corporate sponsors. Corporate sponsors should be looking for us. Grants should come looking for us. Why isn't there a push in Congress, not to create a new accountability system for schools, but one for corporations? Why shouldn't oil companies be forced to provide some of the funds to support a system that supports every organization and business in this world? Oops, I feel a soapbox under my feet.

Kids being "left behind?" I think they are all "9 yielded, 7 correlated, and 8 strategied" out! I know I am. FCAT: Florida Children Are Tired!

If your child hates going to school, or has difficulty "getting to" homework, or if his favorite class is recess, it's time to re-evaluate what's happening. Get involved. I did. Of course, I'm being "realigned." What the heck. All I can say is, "What a ride."

There was a famous industrial study once where a team of "outsiders" came into an industry setting and started to make changes to see how they might be able to improve productivity. They turned up the lighting and productivity increased. They turned down the lighting and productivity increased. No matter what they did, productivity increased. What they eventually determined was that the workers increased their productivity regardless of the conditions because they perceived that management was trying to improve their lot. And so I say, kids are no different. Turn up the light; turn down the light. It's being there consistently, working, worrying, planning, and creating with them. By the way, my kids are both grown and successful in spite of me and because of me. (PS They didn't go into education!)